Morven the Mermaid

retold by Jay Dale

illustrated by Kristina Swarner

Engage Literacy is published in 2013 by Raintree.
Raintree is an imprint of Capstone Global Library Limited, a company
incorporated in Engand and Wales having its registered office at 7 Pilgrim
Street, London, EC4V 6LB – Registered company number: 6695582
www.raintreepublishers.co.uk

Originally published in Australia by Hinkler Education, a division
of Hinkler Books Pty Ltd.
Text copyright © UpLoad Publishing Pty Ltd 2012
Illustration copyright © Hinkler Books Pty Ltd 2012

Written by Jay Dale
Lead authors Jay Dale and Anne Giulieri
Cover illustration and illustrations by Kristina Swarner
Edited by Gwenda Smyth
UK edition edited by Dan Nunn, Catherine Veitch and Sian Smith
Designed by Susannah Low, Butterflyrocket Design

Morvena the Mermaid
ISBN: 978 1 406 26542 2
10 9 8 7 6 5 4

Printed and bound in China by Leo Paper Products Ltd

Contents

Here is an old myth from Cornwall in England...

Chapter 1
A Sad, Sweet Voice

Many years ago in a little village
by the sea, lived a fisherman,
his wife and their three young sons.

The fisherman's name was Lutey
and on summer evenings
he often enjoyed a walk along the beach
with his dog, Towser.

One summer evening, as they strolled
along the beach,
Lutey heard someone crying.

"Oh, no!" came a sad, sweet voice
from behind some rocks.
"I'm stuck here on this rock
and I shall never, ever get home."

Lutey was worried that someone
was in great danger.
So he quickly ran over to where
the voice had come from.
There, sitting all alone on a large rock,
was the most beautiful woman
Lutey had ever seen.

The young woman had long golden hair
that flowed over her shoulders.
She had bright green eyes
that sparkled with tears.
Her hair was held back
by a beautiful pearl comb,
and a seashell necklace
hung around her neck.
But what surprised Lutey most of all
was the silvery fish tail that sparkled
in the afternoon light.

Lutey had discovered a mermaid!

8

Chapter 2
The Beautiful Mermaid

Lutey had heard people say that to look at
a mermaid was dangerous, but the mermaid
was so beautiful he could not turn away.

"Help me!" cried Morvena, the mermaid.
"I was so busy combing my hair
that I didn't notice the tide go out.
Now I am stuck here on this rock.
Please carry me out to the ocean,
so I may swim home to my family
far beneath the sea."

Lutey was a very kind man, so he lifted
the beautiful mermaid in his arms
and carried her towards the deep, blue sea.

Deeper and deeper they went into the ocean,
and soon the water lapped at Lutey's chest.
He gently put Morvena into the ocean
as he looked into her beautiful green eyes.

Morvena did not swim away.
She spoke to him in such a sweet voice
that Lutey could not look away.
"You have been very kind to me," she said,
"and so I will grant you three wishes.
You may have anything you want."

Chapter 3
Three Wishes

Lutey thought for a moment and then replied,
"I do not want things made of gold or silver.
For my first wish, I would like to help
people who are sick.
I want to make them better.
This is my first wish."

He went on, "For my second wish,
I would like to help people who are
fighting with one another.
I want to help them work out
their problems."

Lutey then said, "For my third wish,
I would like my children
and my children's children to help the sick.
I would like them to help people work out
their problems, too."

Morvena smiled and looked straight
into Lutey's eyes.

"Then your three wishes are granted,"
she said.

"Here is my comb for you to keep,
so that you will remember me
and know that I was not a dream."

Morvena was just about to go,
when suddenly she changed her mind.
She began to swim round and round
the fisherman.
"Come with me, Lutey,"
she sang over and over in her sweetest voice.
"Come and live with me far beneath the sea."

Morvena was so beautiful that Lutey
began to follow her deeper and deeper
into the ocean — until only his head
was above the waves.

Suddenly, Lutey heard barking and shouting
from the beach.
He looked away from the beautiful mermaid
to see his dog barking, and his wife
and children calling to him.
Lutey knew what he had to do.
"I cannot go with you," he said to Morvena.
"I belong with my family."

Morvena smiled a strange smile.
"Then," she said, "you will see me
in nine years time."
And she disappeared beneath the waves.

Chapter 4
Nine Years

For nine long years, Lutey lived
a good and happy life.
Sick people came from all around to see him.
Lutey was able to make each one of them
well again.
He also helped people to work out
their problems with one another.
Lutey's boys grew to be strong young men,
and life was good for Lutey and his family.

Then, one summer evening,
nine years after his first meeting
with Morvena, Lutey was out fishing
with his oldest son.

Suddenly, a huge wave came,
tossing the boat up and down in the sea.
Lutey was washed over the side of the boat.
His poor son watched as a beautiful mermaid
with long golden hair took his father's hand.
Then she pulled him down, down, down
to the bottom of the sea.
Lutey the fisherman was never, ever seen again.

23

Over the following years, Lutey's sons
helped to make sick people well again.
They helped people work out their problems,
just as their father had done.

However, every nine years,
one of Lutey's family is lost at sea.
Many say they have gone to join
Lutey and Morvena in their
underwater home beneath the sea.
And there, with Lutey and Morvena,
they live happily ever after.